a minedition book

published by Penguin Young Readers Group

Text copyright © 2007 by Kate Westerlund
Illustrations copyright © 2007 by Eve Tharlet
Original title: Sharing Christmas
Coproduction with Michael Neugebauer Publishing Ltd., Hong Kong.
Rights arranged with "minedition" Rights and Licensing AG,
Zurich, Switzerland.
Published simultaneously in Canada.
Manufactured in China.
Typesetting in Carmina von Gudrun Zapf Hesse.
Color separation by Fotoreproduzioni Grafiche, Verona, Italy.

Library of Congress Cataloging-in-Publication Data available upon request.

ISBN 978-0-698-40074-0
10 9 8 7 6 5 4 3 2 1
First Impression

For more information please visit our website: www.minedition.com

Sharing Christmas

Kate Westerlund

with pictures by Eve Tharlet

minedition

"Look! A shooting star,"
said Clara. "Is it true that every star
in the sky is a wish waiting to come true?"
"I don't know about that," said her mother. "But
I've always thought if you wish for something hard
enough, you can help make it come true."

Then Clara's mother said in a quiet voice,
"Winter has come so early this year.
Too much snow and not enough to eat.
I'm afraid it won't be much of a Christmas...
for anyone."

"Mama, will we have enough to eat?"
asked Clara.
"We'll manage," said her mother. "...somehow."
"And Christmas?" Clara whispered.
But her mother said nothing. She just looked worried.
Clara loved Christmas. There had always been so many surprises.
She wanted it to be the same this year too...for everyone.
So she looked up at the twinkling stars and made a wish.

The next day there was more snow.
That certainly wasn't what Clara had wished for.
Snow made everything so difficult.

In the distance, Clara heard something that sounded like little bells.
"Bells? I've never heard bells here before," she thought.
So she followed the sound.
"Oh, my! What's this?"

"What are you doing?" asked Martin.

"I was following the bells," answered Clara.

"What bells? I don't hear any bells," said Martin.

"I did. And when I followed the sound, I found these," said Clara.

"Berries!" said Martin. "What about nuts? Did you find any nuts?"

"No, I didn't find any nuts," Clara replied sadly.

"Maybe I should come with you in case you find some nuts," said Martin.

"Listen! I think I hear the bells again," said Clara.

"I don't hear …"

"Shhh!" interrupted Clara.

"Hey! Where are you two going?" asked Ralph.

"We're following the bells," answered Martin.

"What bells?" asked Ralph. "Wait, I hear them too. Why are you following the bells?"

"Clara followed the sound of the bells, and then she found some berries," said Martin.

"Can I come with you? Everything I like to eat seems to be buried under snow!" said Ralph.

They all followed the sound of the bells.

"Ouch!" yelled Ralph. "My foot's caught under a branch!"

"How did you do that?" asked Martin.

"I was watching you and not where I was going. Can you help me, please?" asked Ralph.

Martin pushed and Clara pulled.

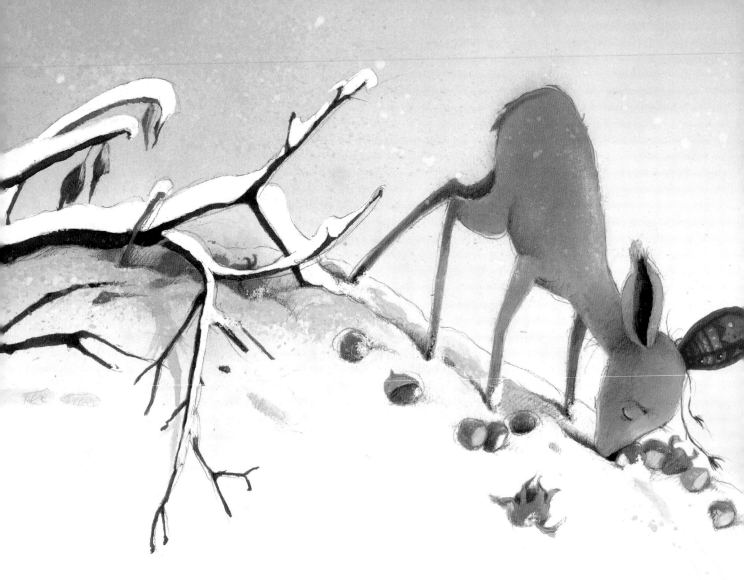

The branch rolled and Ralph's foot was free.
 As it moved, nuts started falling out.
"Oh, boy! Nuts!" cheered Martin.

"Wait! I think we should share these," said Clara.
"Share?" asked Martin.
"With these nuts and berries and maybe something from home…"
 said Clara.
"There isn't very much. Share?" asked Martin again.
"What do you mean — a party?" asked Ralph.
"Yes! A real Christmas celebration," said Clara.

"What's going on?" asked the birds.

"Clara heard bells," said Martin.

"We followed the sound and discovered some wonderful treats! We're going to celebrate," explained Ralph. "Do you want to come too?"

"We have a few seeds we could bring," said the birds. "Can we tell Owl and the others?"

"Of course. Tell everyone!" said Clara. "We'll meet at the bottom of the hill later. We can all go up to the top together. It's the perfect place for a Christmas celebration."

The birds told everyone.
Soon the animals started coming from all parts
of the forest and they each brought something
with them, something for the Christmas celebration,
something to share.

They reached the top of the hill and couldn't believe what they saw. "Oh! Look at the tree," they all said. It was covered with wonderful things to eat and standing next to it was a donkey.

"I'm Osgood," said the donkey,
  the bells on his bridle jingling.
"Your bells!" said Clara. "Did you do all this?"

"The children from the farms have been worried
  that with so much snow you might not have enough
  to eat," said Osgood. "I helped them carry things,
  and they placed the food in different spots so you
  could find it. Then they decorated this tree for Christmas."

"Look at the nuts," said Martin.
"Thank you," sang the birds.
"I overheard the little deer talking about a celebration,"
  said Osgood. "So I brought my carrots."

Suddenly, a glittering star fell from the sky.
Everyone stopped and looked. It was beautiful.

There had never been a Christmas quite like this one.
"Sharing is the best," they all agreed.

"Sharing is giving, and giving is
what Christmas is all about!"